Goodnight Whispers

For my daughter, Willa, and my sons, Jacob and Sam. —M. L.

To Jaume and Mercè, the most caring, supportive and
affectionate parents I can imagine. —D. T.

FAMILIUS

Copyright © 2018 by Michael Leannah.
Illustration Copyright © 2018 by Dani Torrent.

Published by Familius LLC, www.familius.com

Familius books are available at special discounts for bulk purchases, whether for sales promotions or for family or
corporate use. For more information, contact Familius Sales at 559-876-2170 or email orders@familius.com.

Library of Congress Cataloging-in-Publication Data
2018937138   pISBN 9781641700313   eISBN 9781641700658

10 9 8 7 6 5 4 3 2 1
First Edition
Printed in China

GOODNIGHT WHISPERS

MICHAEL
LEANNAH

ILLUSTRATIONS BY
DANI TORRENT

Late one quiet night, a man tiptoed to the side of his daughter's crib. He tucked the edges of the blanket around her tiny feet. He touched his hand to her cheek. He whispered in her ear.

"You are the most wonderful girl in the world."

He stood at the crib the following night.

He whispered, "I can't wait to hold you in my arms again in the morning."

And the next night:

"I love you very much."

The baby grew to be a toddler, and every night the man whispered to her, his voice like a thread stitching a beautifully woven garment.

"Today you fell and hurt yourself, but you got back up and kept climbing to the top of the hill. You are brave and strong."

"You are blossoming like the forget-me-nots we discovered at the edge of the creek."

"I love being your father."

Time went by, and the toddler
became a young girl. She knew how to
do so many things now. Every night
the man whispered to her.
"You climb like a monkey, swim like
an otter, and jump like a kangaroo."

"When you sing, the
world stops to listen."
"Because you're here,
everything is perfect."

The girl became a teenager, and she was like the sun shining high in the sky. She put her heart into everything she did.

"At your soccer game, you ran and kicked until you had no breath left! I was so proud of you."

"I watched you dancing with your friends today. What a joyful dancer you are. What a fun-loving friend!"

"You work and play so hard each day."

When the girl was a
woman, she moved far away.
The man no longer stood
at her bedside, whispering
in the night. But his words
echoed in her dreams,
always finding their way to
her heart.

All through her life she heard her father's goodnight whispers.

When she made a mistake: "You are smart and good."

When frustrations tangled her up: "You will always be okay. You are strong."

When luck turned against her: "Everything will be all right."

The woman trusted her father's voice.

One day the woman got a call. Her father was
ill and needed her help. She and her little son
arrived just as the sun was going down.

Late that night, the man lay
sleeping. His daughter sat at
his side, a photo album open
on her lap.

She studied a picture of
her father. She gazed into
the eyes of her grandmother.
She traced her finger around
a yellow-edged photograph
of her great-grandfather.

She closed the album and
turned out the light.
    She bent and kissed her father's
forehead, then lowered her lips to
his ear.
    "You are the most wonderful
man in the world."

She left the room and
tiptoed to her son's bed,
where he lay quiet and still.
"You are good," she
whispered. "From the top
of your head to the bottom
of your toes, you are so
very, very good."

She slipped into her
own bed and pulled
the covers to her chin.
She drifted off to sleep
to the gentle whispers
of the night.